# The Albatross

Scott Lauder and Walter McGregor

# About this Book

## For the Student

🎧 Listen to the story and do some activities on your Audio CD
🎧 End of the listening excerpt
💬 Talk about the story
ban° When you see the blue dot you can check the word in the glossary
🅿 Prepare for Cambridge English: Preliminary (PET) for Schools

## For the Teacher

 A state-of-the-art interactive learning environment with 1000s of free online self-correcting activities for your chosen readers.

Go to our Readers Resource site for information on using readers and downloadable Resource Sheets, photocopiable Worksheets and Answer Keys. Plus free sample tracks from the story.

www.helblingreaders.com
For lots of great ideas on using Graded Readers consult Reading Matters, the Teacher's Guide to using Helbling Readers.

### Level 5 Structures

| | |
|---|---|
| Modal verb would | Non-defining relative clauses |
| I'd love to ... | Present perfect continuous |
| Future continuous | Used to / would |
| Present perfect future | Used to / used to doing |
| Reported speech / verbs / questions | Second conditional |
| Past perfect | Expressing wishes and regrets |
| Defining relative clauses | |

Structures from other levels are also included.

# Contents

| | | |
|---|---|---:|
| Meet the Authors | | 6 |
| Before Reading | | 7 |
| 1 | "But that's impossible" | 13 |
| 2 | "We have a problem" | 16 |
| 3 | "A falcon" | 21 |
| 4 | "There's something you need to see" | 26 |
| 5 | "I'm sorry, Dad" | 28 |
| 6 | "He's nervous... but the question is: why?" | 32 |
| 7 | "We bring the birds, he brings the cash" | 36 |
| 8 | "Murder wasn't part of the deal" | 40 |
| 9 | "He was dead!" | 46 |
| 10 | "The shoes!" | 51 |
| 11 | "If I am cursed, then he is lucky" | 56 |
| 12 | "My wife's name was Karis" | 59 |
| 13 | "Eventually, we feel grateful" | 62 |
| 14 | "It's been a long time" | 66 |
| After Reading | | 69 |

# HELBLING DIGITAL

**THE EDUCATIONAL PLATFORM**

**HELBLING e-zone is an inspiring new state-of-the-art, easy-to-use interactive learning environment.**

The online self-correcting activities include:
- reading comprehension;
- listening comprehension;
- vocabulary;
- grammar;
- exam preparation.

▪ **TEACHERS** register free of charge to set up classes and assign individual and class homework sets. Results are provided automatically once the deadline has been reached and detailed reports on performance are available at a click.

▪ **STUDENTS** test their language skills in a stimulating interactive environment. All activities can be attempted as many times as necessary and full results and feedback are given as soon as the deadline has been reached. Single student access is also available.

# FREE INTERACTIVE ONLINE TEACHING AND LEARNING MATERIALS

1000s of free online interactive activities now available for HELBLING READERS and your other favorite Helbling Languages publications.

### www.helbling-ezone.com
ONLINE ACTIVITIES

# blog.helblingreaders.com

**NEW**

Love reading and readers and can't wait to get your class interested? Have a class library and reading program, but not sure how to take it a step further? The Helbling Readers BLOG is the place for you.

The **Helbling Readers BLOG** will provide you with ideas on setting up and running a Book Club and tips on reading lessons **every week**.

- Book Club
- Worksheets
- Lesson Plans

**Subscribe** to our **BLOG** and you will never miss out on our updates.

# Meet the Authors

### Can you tell us a little about yourselves?
**Scott:** I am doing a doctorate• in Education, so I don't get much time for hobbies. However, I do like to read fiction. At the moment, I am reading Patrick O'Brian. He wrote twenty-one books about Captain Aubrey, but I wish there were more. **Walter:** I love writing short stories, but my business keeps me very busy. I live in Scotland and I work there, too, so I often go hill-walking.
My other hobbies are playing guitar and sketching•.

### How did you two meet?
**Walter:** We met at primary school many years ago!

### Have you written together before?
**Scott:** Yes! We've written more than twenty stories so far.

### How does writing a book together work?
**Walter:** Usually, one of us will have an idea and then we will talk about it. Because Scott lives in the UAE• and I am in Scotland, we chat on the computer a lot!

### Does the book have a message?
**Scott:** I think the book is partly about grief•. When someone important in our lives dies, we have to remember that person, but we also have to move forward.

### Where did you get the idea for this story?
**Walter:** Scott and I were sitting in a café next to the ocean. It was a cold, wet, windy night. As we looked out of the café's window, we saw the lights of a boat in the Firth of Clyde•. What was the boat carrying, we wondered•...

### Any more stories in the future?
**Scott and Walter:** Lots!

---

### Glossary

- **doctorate:** highest qualification from a university
- **Firth of Clyde:** area of ocean on the southwest coast of Scotland
- **grief:** sadness when someone dies
- **sketching:** drawing
- **UAE:** United Arab Emirates
- **wondered:** asked ourselves

# BEFORE READING

1 *The Albatross* is the name of the cargo ship where different parts of the story are set. Look at this picture of a cargo ship and then use the words from the story in the box below to label the picture. Use a dictionary if necessary.

deck    stairwell    hold    hull    galley

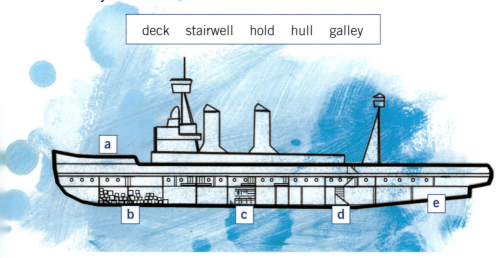

2 These people all work on a ship. What do they do?
Write a definition with a partner. Use a dictionary to help you.

captain    crew    engineer

| People on a ship | What they do |
|---|---|
|  |  |
|  |  |

3 What is an albatross? Work with a partner. Write down some reasons why you think the ship is called *The Albatross*.

# BEFORE READING

🎧 **1 Read and complete the following introductions to some of the characters in the story, using the words below. Then listen and check your answers.**

| soccer   crazy   Police   Haven   two   Pip   afternoon   sixteen |
|---|

**a)** My name's Molly Mundy and I'm **1** ................... years old. I come from a small town called **2** ..................., which is on the east coast of the United States. I have a dog called **3** ................... . My hobbies include playing **4** ................... and going for walks on the beach. I live with my father, who works for Haven Harbor **5** ................... . Apart from my dog, there are just **6** ................... of us in our house, although my aunt often comes to visit in the **7** ...................: my dad thinks I need a babysitter and that makes me **8** ...................!

| retire   sixty-five   brother   Levy   engineer   Greece |
|---|

**b)** My name's Leveros Andreas, but everyone calls me **1** ................... . I'm **2** ................... years old and I work as a ship's **3** ................... . The voyage on *The Albatross* is my last one. After it finishes, I plan to **4** ................... . I want to go back to **5** ..................., buy a small boat and go fishing with my **6** ................... .

| ship   engineer   work   prison |

**c)** My name's Carlos. Who cares where I come from? I met Andre while we were both in **1** ................. . Andre is an idiot, but we always seem to **2** ................. together. We met the captain of *The Albatross* in Malta. I didn't trust the captain then and I don't trust him now! Levy's okay and he's a good **3** ................. to have on the **4** ................., but he's old and wants everything to be perfect all the time.

| years   Shell   Dan   four   widower |

**d)** My name's Lieutenant Daniel Mundy, but my friends call me **1** ................. . I have been a lieutenant for almost **2** ................. years and I'm hoping to get a promotion soon. I work in Haven, but I live with my daughter, Molly, in a small house near **3** ................. Bay. I'm a **4** ................. , since my wife died a few **5** ................. ago. Having a wonderful daughter like Molly makes things easier.

**2** Read Exercise 1 again. Use the information to complete the sentences with the correct names.

a) Pip belongs to ........................... .
b) ........................... is Dan Mundy's daughter.
c) The captain, Levy, Andre, and ........................... work on *The Albatross*.
d) ........................... is Carlos's friend, but Carlos thinks he is an idiot.
e) ........................... is the ship's engineer on *The Albatross*.
f) ........................... 's mother died a few years ago.
g) ........................... doesn't trust the captain.
h) ........................... and Carlos have been in prison.

9

# BEFORE READING

**1** Look at these action verbs from the story. What do they mean? Use a dictionary if necessary. When we do the action, do we usually use all of our body or part of our body or both? What do you think? Complete the table and check (✔) either 'All', 'Part' or 'Both'. Mime the actions with a partner.

| Action | All | Part | Both |
|---|---|---|---|
| **a)** step | | | |
| **b)** lean | | | |
| **c)** nod | | | |
| **d)** tighten | | | |
| **e)** sprint | | | |
| **f)** glance | | | |
| **g)** shrug | | | |
| **h)** rush | | | |
| **i)** dash | | | |
| **j)** swallow | | | |
| **k)** wink | | | |

**2** Use some of the verbs from Exercise 1 to ask and answer these questions with a partner. Make questions for three other verbs and ask another pair.

**a)** What would you do if you were in a hurry?

**b)** What would you do if you agreed with someone?

**c)** What would you do if you wanted to look at something quickly?

**d)** What would you do if you were eating?

**e)** What would you do if you didn't know the answer?

**f)** What would you do if you were telling a joke?

**3** Use the words below to complete these sentences.

> nodded   stepped   sprinted   swallow

a) Levy ................ forward but then jumped back. It wasn't a rat at his feet, it was an apple core.

b) The captain ................ slowly. 'Of course,' he replied. 'You're right.'

c) Levy felt thirsty. He tried to ................, but couldn't. Molly filled a glass of water for him.

d) Pip gave Molly a quick look and ................ down the hill toward Shell Bay: his favorite place.

**4** Look at the pictures below. What can you see? Tell a friend.

# 1 "But that's impossible"

The Albatross wasn't the most beautiful ship in the world, but Leveros Andreas didn't care. He was the ship's engineer ● and everybody knew him as Levy. At sixty-five and after almost fifty years at sea, this was his final voyage. He couldn't wait to retire ● and use the money he had saved to buy a house in his home town of Nikiti, in Greece. He and the other two members of the crew ● were sailing toward the harbor town of Haven with their cargo ● of televisions. This was Levy's first time on The Albatross, but not his first time to visit Haven. Years before, when his wife was still alive, he had visited the little harbor town on the east coast of the United States with her. Those were happy years.

Levy looked at the gold watch that his wife had given him for his 40th birthday. "1:14!" he said. Usually, he tried to be in bed by twelve; but Herman, the ship's cat, was missing. There was a storm coming and he was worried. "I'll murder that cat when I find him!" he said, shaking his head.

There was only one more place to check: the cargo deck ●. He began climbing down the stairs to the lowest deck. He had almost reached ● the bottom step when he stopped. There, in front of him, the door to the cargo room lay ● half open. It was dark inside. Normally, the door was locked for security ● reasons. Levy thought about going to tell the captain immediately, but then he thought about Herman.

"Hermaaaan! Hey, Hermaaaan," Levy called from the door of the hold ●. "Are you in there?" He pulled out his flashlight.

"Hermaaaaan!" Levy called again. The flashlight shined only a few feet through the door and into the darkness, but Levy didn't really want to go any farther. The truth was he was frightened of rats. This was one of the reasons why he liked Herman.

## Glossary

- **cargo:** things that a ship carries
- **crew:** people who work on a ship
- **deck:** area or level on a ship
- **engineer:** (here) person who works with engines
- **hold:** large area for cargo
- **lay:** (here) was; remained
- **reached:** arrived at
- **retire:** stop working because he is old
- **security:** safety

Levy stood still. The ship was beginning to rise and fall more quickly now: the storm was getting closer.

"Herrrrr-maaaaaan, where are you?" Levy called out.

The captain's orders were that no one was allowed to go into the cargo hold but Levy had to find Herman. Hesitantly •, Levy stepped • forward but he touched something with his foot. He jumped back and looked down. An apple core • lay at his feet.
At least it wasn't a rat.

"Andre!" thought Levy. Andre was always leaving these things lying around. He pictured Andre's face. "Large" and "stupid" were the words that immediately came into his mind. Andre and his friend, Carlos, were his two crewmates •. Although it wasn't easy on a small ship, Levy tried to stay away from them as much as possible.

"I should get out of here," he thought. "That crazy cat will have to find his own way out: I need to go and tell the captain about this door."

"Kkkkeeeeeeeeeew!"

The sound came from somewhere in the darkness.

"Keeeeew! Keeeeeeew!"

## The sound
**What do YOU think makes this sound?**

### Glossary

- **core:** center
- **crewmates:** people who work on the same ship
- **hesitantly:** nervously; anxiously
- **moth:** butterfly-like insect which flies at night
- **path:** route; way
- **piled high:** a lot of things on top of each other
- **stepped:** moved

# The Albatross

"What was that?" he whispered to himself. He shined his flashlight into the darkness and moved toward the sound. The sound came again, only louder. Hundreds of boxes were piled high• on both sides of him; but there was a clear path• through them, like a river through a canyon. Levy's mouth fell open. At the far end of the hold, a light came from a half-open door. "But that's impossible," he said. "There are no other rooms in the cargo hold."

But there was another room and there was another light and it was drawing Levy forward like a moth• toward a lamp.

## 2 "We have a problem"

Outside the room, Levy stopped. He could feel his heart beating hard. He switched off his flashlight and leaned • his head through the narrow doorway. The first thing he saw was a large sheet • covering something. He stepped into the room. There were sheets everywhere.

With one hand he reached forward and, taking the nearest sheet, he pulled it off.

A beautiful falcon with shining eyes stared • back at him from its cage.

"What on earth…? • " he said and reached for the other sheets. Under each one, there were more birds. In all, Levy counted nearly forty cages with one and sometimes two falcons in each. He was furious. These birds were special. There were laws to protect them from men like Andre. He thought about the police. "If they find the birds, it'll mean trouble for all of us. I need to see the captain."

Picking up the nearest cage, he walked out of the hold and back up the stairs to the captain's room. He knocked on the door and went straight in.

Inside, the captain was sitting at a small desk, his ear to a cell phone. His big body made the room seem even smaller than it was.

"What's going on? • " he asked sharply • when Levy walked in.

"I'm sorry to disturb you," replied Levy, "but I found this in the hold," and he held up the cage.

The captain stared at the falcon. "I'll call you back," he said into his cell phone. His dark eyes turned back to Levy. "What were you doing in the hold?" he asked.

"I was looking for Herman," answered Levy, "and I found this. There are more than forty cages down there."

---

### Glossary

- **leaned:** pushed forward
- **sharply:** harshly; impolitely
- **sheet:** piece of material
- **stared:** looked at in a fixed way
- **What on earth?:** exclamation of surprise
- **What's going on?:** What's happening?

Silence.

"It's Andre," Levy continued. "He's responsible."

"Andre? What makes you think it's him?"

"I found an apple…"

"…and that means it's Andre?" the captain asked, a strange smile on his face.

Levy didn't understand: this was serious. "Captain," he said, "these are rare• birds; we could all go to jail for this."

The captain seemed lost in thought. Levy spoke again. "Call the police," he said, "before they come onto the ship and find the birds for themselves."

The captain nodded• slowly. "Of course," he replied. "You're right." He moved around the table and put his arm around Levy's shoulder. "I'll call them. Don't worry, everything's going to be fine. Okay?"

Levy nodded. "Okay", he said, beginning to relax. "I'll take the bird to my room." The captain nodded and Levy opened the door. "Thank you, captain," he said.

As soon as the door was closed and Levy was gone, the captain quickly called someone on his cell phone.

"We have a problem," said the captain.

Levy was walking along the corridor that led to his room. He wanted to put the falcon somewhere safe. All of a sudden Herman ran past, tail in the air.

"Hey," shouted Levy. "Where are you going?" But Herman didn't stop. He continued at full speed• and disappeared down the corridor. Levy laughed to himself. "Unbelievable! I thought birds were supposed to be scared of cats."

---

### Glossary

- **at full speed:** as fast as he could
- **nodded:** moved his head to show that he agreed
- **rare:** not common (there are not many of them)

## The Albatross

Then Levy heard a noise behind him. He turned around quickly. Carlos and Andre stood a few feet away, both of them staring coldly at him. They looked big and heavy in their overalls •.

"Going somewhere?" asked Carlos.

"To my room," replied Levy.

Carlos smiled. He looked at the cage and said, "You have something that isn't yours."

Levy felt threatened •. He was too old to fight these two big guys. He tried to think of a way to get past them.

"Do you know what time it is?" asked Andre suddenly.

Levy looked at his watch: almost 1:32 A.M. Suddenly, a sharp pain filled Levy's head and everything went dark for a second. When he opened his eyes he was lying on the floor, but he was still holding the cage.

"You should give Carlos the falcon, old man," Andre said threateningly from behind Carlos's shoulder.

Carlos pushed his face close to Levy's. When he spoke, the smell of his breath filled Levy's nose. "Don't make me hurt you, old man," he whispered, his green eyes shining.

"Captain…" cried out Levy, "Captain!"

In an instant, Carlos's hand was around Levy's throat; the other across his mouth.

"Stupid old man…" whispered Carlos. Andre grabbed the cage and tried to tear • it from Levy's hand. The cage fell backward and crashed against the stairs that led to the deck above. The door of the cage swung open •.

---

- **overalls:** type of working clothes
- **swung open:** opened wide
- **tear:** take with violence
- **threatened:** (here) scared; they might hurt him

"Catch it!" shouted Carlos, reaching out an arm. But it was too late. The falcon disappeared through the open door above them and into the night. A second later, the men turned back to Levy. Carlos's fists• tightened•.

Andre knocked on the captain's door. Beside him, Carlos was rubbing his fists.

"Come in."

The men stepped inside.

"Well?" asked the captain.

Carlos and Andre looked at one another. "We had a slight• problem," said Carlos.

The captain stood up. "I know you had a problem!"

"Levy let the bird go," Andre lied.

The captain slammed• his hand on the desk. "That's one thousand dollars lost! You idiots!"

Andre looked at the floor, but Carlos's eyes blazed•.

"Where is he?" continued the captain. "Where did you put him?"

"Don't worry, we took care of• him," replied Carlos.

"We gave him a bath," laughed Andre like a child. "Man overboard•!"

The captain sat down again and looked out of the small window. A black sky greeted him. The old man was never part of their plans and now he was dead. Fine! But if the police found his body quickly they would be in trouble. The police would know that the old man hadn't drowned.

"Don't worry. We've seen the last of him•," said Carlos, reading the captain's thoughts.

"I hope so," the captain said. "I certainly hope so."

## Glossary

- **blazed:** burned brightly
- **fists:** closed hands
- **man overboard:** when someone falls in the sea
- **seen the last of him:** won't see him again
- **slammed:** hit very hard
- **slight:** minor; not serious
- **tightened:** closed firmly
- **took care of:** managed

### 3 "A falcon"

Sixteen-year-old Molly Mundy stood beside her bed in a long, white shirt and rubbed her eyes. Her hair was a mess •, and she felt horrible. A storm had woken her up at 3 A.M., and she hadn't fallen asleep again for ages.

When she looked at her alarm clock, she groaned. Today was Monday, Memorial Day • Monday, and she was wide awake at exactly 7 A.M. She turned and looked at Pip who was watching her with excited eyes. "Why did I forget to close my bedroom door last night?" she asked herself. Pip was her dog and she loved him... except when he came into her room and woke her up with a cold, wet nose pressed against her face.

She pulled open the curtains and looked outside. The air was clear and there was almost no wind. "I guess I have no excuse, huh?" she asked Pip. Watching his wagging tail, she slipped on • a pair of jeans and pushed her dark hair under her old New York Cosmos cap.

## Cap

**Do you know what New York Cosmos is?**
**Do some research on the Internet to find out.**
**Why do you think Molly has a New York Cosmos cap?**
**Do you have a special cap or T-shirt?**

▷◁ **Tell a friend.**

---

- **Memorial Day:** in USA, the last Monday in May, when all the people who died in the US armed forces are remembered
- **mess:** not tidy
- **slipped on:** (here) put on quickly

21

"Okay," Molly said. "Let's go."

Immediately, Pip was at her side, following her down the stairs and into the living room. She pulled on a pair of white sports shoes and called into the kitchen.

"I'm taking Pip over to Shell Bay •," she said.

"Did you have your breakfast?" her father called back.

"Um…Won't be long,' replied Molly.

"Hey, you got a key? I'm leaving for work soon," her father said.

"Yup •!"

"Have some breakfast when you come back, okay?"

"Okay, bye," replied Molly, and with Pip pushing past her, she stepped out of the door.

Shell Bay lay to the north of her house, a wide C-shaped line of yellow sand that ran for three miles up the coast toward the harbor at Haven. It was a fifteen-minute walk from her house over the hills to the beach, but she loved going there. Others from Haven sometimes went there, too, but she guessed the beach would be empty at this time.

At the top of the hill, Molly turned and looked back. Her father waved to her and she waved back. She watched him get in his car and leave for work. Soon, the car was out of sight •, traveling north along Highway 12 to Haven. Her dad worked for Haven Harbor Police and Molly often worried about him, just like her mother used to do. After her mother died two years ago, Molly tried to help out as much as possible: making shopping lists, doing the housework, ironing her dad's shirts, those kinds of things. And walking Pip.

## Glossary

- **bay:** place on coast where the land curves inward
- **out of sight:** no longer visible
- **yup:** yes

Pip gave Molly a quick look and sprinted• down the hill to the beach. Molly held on to her cap and ran, too. Soon, they were both walking beside the sparkling• water. After a while, Molly picked up a stick• and was about to throw it when she saw a bird flying to the north. "A falcon," she whispered. The bird flew overhead•. She followed it with her eyes, turning to watch until it was too small to see. Then Molly threw the stick for Pip. It fell somewhere on the other side of an old tree trunk• that lay near the water. Immediately, Pip went running after it. When he reached the tree trunk, he leaped• over it and disappeared from sight. Molly began walking slowly toward him, taking deep breaths of the fresh morning air. A ship that was slowly moving in the direction of Haven caught her eye. "Glad I wasn't on that," she thought, remembering the storm from last night.

Now Pip was barking loudly. She smiled. "He's lost the stick," she thought and began looking for another one. Then she saw it: something shiny in the sand. She reached down and picked it up. It was a watch, a gold watch. The time on it said 1:38. She turned it over. On the back, there was writing, but she couldn't understand it. "What language is that?" she wondered•.

Pip was now barking madly. "What's the matter with him?" She could just see his tail from behind the large tree trunk. "What is he so excited about?" She could see his head above the tree trunk now. He was running around, but his eyes were fixed on something behind the tree trunk.

Molly came closer… She stood and stared in horror.

An old man lay against the side of the tree trunk, his face to the sky. Molly turned and ran as fast as she could back along the beach. Pip was at her heels.

### Glossary

- **leaped:** jumped
- **overhead:** above
- **sparkling:** shining in the light
- **sprinted:** ran at full speed
- **stick:** thin piece of wood from a tree
- **tree trunk:** main part of a tree
- **wondered:** thought

## Molly
What four things does Molly see or find that are linked to the first part of the story?

# 4 "There's something you need to see"

Morning sunshine was pouring • in through the cabin's only window. Its yellow light fell on the captain's broad back and his black uniform. With his laptop open in front of him, he sat silently with his eyes on the screen. Andre and Carlos were sitting opposite him. They were watching every move of his face.

It was the morning after the storm and the ship was sailing calmly on a sea of blue. They were near Haven now. In a few hours they could deliver the birds and get their money.

"That was a good storm last night," said Andre, to no one in particular. "Shame • our engineer didn't enjoy it!"

Carlos looked at Andre coolly.

Andre smiled, showing a row of brown teeth. "Relax!" he said. "I know the story: the old man was sick. He fell over the side. We tried to save him, but we couldn't reach him... Then the captain made a distress call • to the Coast Guard •."

"Be quiet! Both of you," said the captain. "If the police find him now, we'll spend the next twenty years in prison. Think about THAT!" His words hung in the air for several moments. He switched off his laptop just as his cell phone rang. He answered it and at once began shouting.

Andre leaned over to Carlos. "Hopper?" he whispered. Carlos nodded.

"Wait," the captain told the caller. He stared at Andre and Carlos. "Go on deck and keep watch."

Andre and Carlos stood up and left the cabin. Behind them, they could hear the call with Hopper continue. Andre whistled happily as he climbed the stairs to the deck.

## Glossary

- **Coast Guard:** armed police that guard the coast
- **distress call:** emergency call
- **pouring:** shining; flooding
- **shame:** pity

# The Albatross

Carlos, however, was far from happy. He didn't like the way the captain spoke to him; but most of all, he didn't like the way the money, the $60,000 for the falcons, was divided. Why should the captain get fifty percent? Why should he and Andre each get twenty-five percent? Up on deck, he was still deep in thought when Andre pushed the powerful binoculars in front of his face.

"There's something you need to see," he said, pointing to a nearby beach. Carlos took the binoculars. "I don't believe it..." he said.

"Captain's not going to like this," said Andre.

Like green flames, Carlos's eyes turned on him. "I told you to put him in chains•. Did you?"

Andre stared stupidly at Carlos. "There was some old rope..." he began to reply.

"Did you take out his ID•?"

Andre said nothing, but a look of panic crossed his face.

"You idiot!'" hissed• Carlos.

"I forgot! There was too much to do. He was heavy and I couldn't..."

"Shut up!" Carlos shouted. He had to think. Levy wasn't deep beneath them at the bottom of the ocean; he was lying on the beach like a sunbather. Even worse, he still had his ID in his pocket. He knew he had to tell the captain and admit his mistake: he had told Andre to take care of Levy instead of doing it himself. But right now, there was only one thing to do: they had to get the old man's body off the beach and hide it somewhere on the ship.

"Get the boat," Carlos said. "Bring the old man back on board and put his body in the hold."

Mouth open, Andre stood and stared.

"Get...the...boat," repeated Carlos slowly. "Now!"

---

- **hissed:** whispered angrily
- **ID:** identification
- **in chains:** tied up using metal links

## 5 "I'm sorry, Dad"

For hours, the police had gone up and down the beach searching for the body, but they had found nothing. Molly looked toward the trail • that led over the hill. One after the other, the officers disappeared over the top of the hill. The last to vanish were the two paramedics • who were carrying the empty stretcher •.

In front of her, staring out at the ocean, her father stood on the beach in his gray harbor police shirt and pants. The hat that he was wearing made him seem even taller and thinner.

"I'm sorry, Dad," Molly finally said, taking his hand and looking up at him. She didn't know what else to say. There had been a body. She had seen an old man lying dead on the sand. But now that body wasn't there. It had disappeared... it didn't make sense.

"It's not your fault •," he said. "I... I haven't been there for you •, not really." He looked down at her, "Not after Mom died." His eyes were soft and kind. "Anyway, I was thinking of taking a few days off work...going to the Big Apple •." He smiled. "We could see a show • and stay at Grandma and Grandpa's."

Molly smiled, too. Her father was born in Haven, but her mother came from New York; and her grandparents still lived there, in the same house on Riverside Drive that her mother was born in. She loved visiting the Big Apple, especially Broadway •. She missed that. She also missed staying with her grandparents. Since her mother's death, she and her father hadn't stayed there once.

---

### Glossary

- **been there for you:** been ready to help you
- **Big Apple:** New York City
- **Broadway:** area in New York City with many theaters
- **paramedics:** emergency doctors
- **show:** musical or play
- **stretcher:** cloth bed for carrying sick or injured people
- **trail:** rough path across hills or in forests
- **your fault:** your responsibility

# The Albatross

But the reason for the trip • wasn't hard to guess. It was because of today. She guessed that her father thought the 'body on the beach' was a cry for attention, that she imagined the whole thing. She didn't blame him • .

She squeezed • his hand.

"Listen, I have to go back to the office," he said gently. "But I'll be back home around five, okay?"

"Yeah," said Molly, nodding. "Okay."

"You got practice • today?"

Molly shook her head. Haven High was district soccer • champion and Molly was the girls' team captain. "That was yesterday," she said.

"Yesterday..." Her father nodded. "Of course."

"What about the watch?" Molly asked.

"The watch?"

Molly pulled the watch from the back pocket of her jeans.

Her father glanced • at it. With his hand on her shoulder, they turned around and began walking toward the start of the trail.

"Well," said her father, "I guess somebody dropped it. Why don't you keep it for now and we'll put an ad • in Marty's store window?"

Molly turned the watch over in her hands. "The inscription • is in Russian... or something," she said. Her father, however, wasn't paying attention. Instead, he was looking out at the ocean. He was still looking there when Molly saw the falcon from earlier in the day. Now it was just above the top of the hill in front of them.

"Dad..." she said. But as soon as she said it, the bird dropped out of sight and was gone.

"Hmmm?" asked her father, turning toward her "What?"

"Oh, nothing," replied Molly.

---

- **ad:** advertisement
- **didn't blame him:** (here) could understand (why he thought that)
- **glanced:** looked at quickly
- **inscription:** written message (often on stone or metal)
- **practice:** training
- **soccer:** football
- **squeezed:** pressed
- **trip:** short vacation

They walked on in silence. Her father put his arm around Molly and pulled her close to him.

"Is Aunt Ellie coming over today?" Molly asked. Aunt Ellie was her father's older sister. Her father didn't like Molly being in the house by herself, too young, he said, so Aunt Ellie usually came later in the afternoon and stayed a few hours.

Her father nodded.

"But Dad, I'm sixteen. I don't need a babysitter."

Her father smiled. "You're still my little girl."

That made Molly want to scream, but instead she ran ahead to the top of the hill.

In the distance, above the sound of the waves and the wind, the falcon's call rang out.

# The Albatross

As soon as she got home, Molly went up to her room, with Pip following closely behind her. On her bed, she read the name on the back of the watch again: "L-e-v-e-r-o-s." She thought again about the body on the beach. She had no idea why, but she felt there was a connection. She looked at Pip: the body's disappearance, and the words on the watch were of no interest to him at all. Instead, he was curled up• at the foot of the bed, his eyes already beginning to close. She smiled. Her aunt Ellie was not coming until later in the afternoon and Molly didn't have school or soccer practice to go to. She had plenty of time to do a little research before she had breakfast and did some chores• around the house.

She switched on her laptop. She typed the words from the back of the watch into Google translator. A moment later, the translation appeared. She repeated the words slowly: "To my darling Leveros 'Levy' Andreas. All my love, K."

The watch was a present from someone. It meant that the old man might be someone's grandfather, someone's uncle, or even someone's husband…

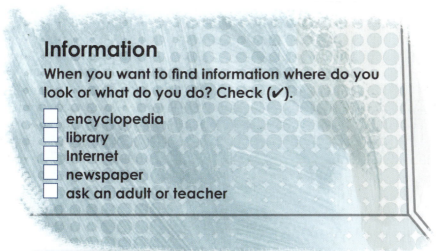

## Information

When you want to find information where do you look or what do you do? Check (✔).

- [ ] encyclopedia
- [ ] library
- [ ] Internet
- [ ] newspaper
- [ ] ask an adult or teacher

### Glossary

- **curled up:** with his legs pulled very close to his body
- **chores:** daily jobs in the house

## 6 "He's nervous... but the question is: why?"

Lieutenant Daniel Mundy had just spent two useless hours on a beach near his home looking for a dead body. After the search, he had returned to the office and written a report. Then he had gone to the police cafeteria for a late lunch. He was having coffee, his first of the day, when his boss came to his table. "A cargo ship has just come in, Dan," his boss had said. In reply, Mundy had felt like saying, "get someone else to check it," but he hadn't. It was part of his job.

Now it was 2:40 P.M. and he was standing below deck, documents in one hand, flashlight in the other, carrying out his usual inspection of cargo. But a voice in his head was growing louder and louder all the time. Something about the hold and this man's behavior was not right…

He turned to the man who was escorting• him. "How many TVs are you carrying?" he asked, switching on the flashlight.

"Sorry•?" asked the captain. The noise from the ship's engines and the generators was loud and it was difficult to hear anyone unless they shouted. Lieutenant Mundy repeated his question and shined the flashlight through the door of the hold. Box after box greeted him as he moved his flashlight around the room.

"Eight hundred and fifteen," the captain replied, standing stiffly• at the door.

Lieutenant Mundy nodded slowly.

"That's all," the captain added.

"There it was again: something in the man's voice that was… odd," thought Lieutenant Mundy. "I see," he said, switching off his flashlight.

### Glossary

- **escorting:** accompanying
- **Sorry?:** excuse me; I don't understand
- **stiffly:** rigidly; not relaxed

# The Albatross

Lieutenant Mundy stepped past *The Albatross*'s captain. "Are you sure this is all you have?" he asked, taking the customs documents • from his pocket. He kept his eyes fixed on the man's heavy face.

"You've seen all of the ship," replied the captain.

"That doesn't mean I've seen everything, does it?" Lieutenant Mundy asked. He smiled, but the captain did not return it.

"He's nervous," Lieutenant Mundy thought, "but the question is: why?" He began filling in the documents. Beside the word *Cargo*, he wrote 'TVs'; next to *Number*, he wrote '815.' "So, how long will you be staying in Haven?" he asked.

"A few days. Two perhaps."

Lieutenant Mundy nodded. He studied the captain's face. Experience was a good teacher. After twenty years of working in Haven Harbor Police, Dan Mundy had met all kinds of people. Sometimes the lies they told were for stupid reasons, but most of the time people lied because they were breaking the law. "How many are in the crew?" he asked.

The captain stood as still as a statue.

"Myself and three others. But as you probably know, the engineer was sadly lost."

Lieutenant Mundy stared at the man. "What did you say?" he asked.

"We lost a man at sea… I've already reported it to the Coast Guard."

"When?" asked Lieutenant Mundy.

"Last night, around 3 A.M."

When Lieutenant Mundy had arrived at the office that morning, it had been quiet. Today was Memorial Day and reports from other agencies such as the Coast Guard took longer than usual to reach his desk. Even so, he was angry: he should have known about this sooner.

---

• **customs documents:** official documents for the cargo on the ship

Pictures of Molly telling him over and over that she had seen a body on the beach filled his head. "I see. I'm sorry to hear that. Did you know him well?"

"No," replied the captain, "hardly at all. Our regular engineer became sick just before the voyage started so… bad luck, eh?"

"What was the new engineer's name?"

"Eh… Leveros Andreas," replied the captain, "but we called him Levy. Nice man… very sad."

Lieutenant Mundy nodded. "Was he young?"

The captain shook his head. "He was an old guy, Greek… I gave the details already."

"Right," said Lieutenant Mundy, "I'm sure you did. Well, I think everything is fine here. Can you just sign this, please?" He passed the customs documents to the captain. The captain signed and returned them.

"I hope you have a pleasant time in Haven," Lieutenant Mundy said.

A faint smile crossed the captain's face.

# The Albatross

Molly reached for the home phone and picked it up.

"Hi honey," said Molly's father into his cell phone. "You busy?"

"No, just making dinner. Aunt Ellie is here."

"Great! Listen… the reason I'm calling is I want to apologize about earlier… I don't know what's going on, but I think you were right."

"About what?" asked Molly.

"I think you did see someone on the beach. In fact, I'm sure of it. I just wanted to say I was sorry…"

"It's okay," Molly interrupted. "It was kind of weird. I mean one minute there was a body on the beach and the next minute, it's gone."

"Yeah, well, anyway. I just wanted to say I was sorry, okay?"

"Okay," replied Molly.

"By the way, did you say the person that you saw was pretty old?"

"Yeah," replied Molly, "probably near seventy. I mean with his gray hair and…"

"Right, that's all I wanted to know. See you later…" Her father was about to end the call, but Molly stopped him.

"Dad, wait," she said. "Do you think the watch belonged to him?"

"What watch?" he asked.

"The one I found on the beach this morning. You know, the one with the writing on the back. I found out what the inscription said: it's Greek. The watch belonged to someone called Andreas…"

# 7 "We bring the birds, he brings the cash"

The three men were sitting around a table in the ship's galley •. Only ten minutes had passed since the visit from the harbor police, but the captain of *The Albatross* had already forgotten the lieutenant's name. When Carlos asked him about what had happened, the captain shrugged •: "The cop • asked a few questions, nothing to worry about," he said.

"So what happens now?" asked Carlos.

"Hopper," said the captain, "wants me to meet him later in town. The deal • is arranged for 4 A.M. We bring the birds, he brings the cash •."

Hopper was the man who bought the animals that they smuggled •, and he only wanted to deal with • the captain. That made Carlos mad. Why should the captain get $30,000? Was his job twice as dangerous? Was he twice as smart? "There must be some way to make Hopper trust me," thought Carlos. "I need to get Hopper's number, or..." Slowly, another plan began to form in his head. Andre finished eating his apple and wiped his mouth with his sleeve. "What about the police?" he asked, moving his eyes from the captain's face to Carlos's.

"What about them?" asked the captain.

"Are they coming back?"

"Perhaps. I showed them the hold and our passports, but they'll want to check all of our stories about Levy," replied the captain, getting to his feet.

"Why are you going to see Hopper by yourself?" asked Carlos suddenly.

For a moment, the captain was too surprised to say anything and a silence fell. Then he let out a deep breath and smiled coldly. "It's very simple: Hopper is a very nervous man; and you, my friend, make him even more nervous."

---

### Glossary

- **cash:** money
- **cop**: police officer
- **deal:** business agreement
- **deal with:** do business with
- **galley:** kitchen
- **shrugged:** showed (with shoulders) he didn't care
- **smuggled:** moved illegally

Although it was late afternoon, the sun was still shining brightly and the air was hot. Molly, however, was walking beneath the trees. She was enjoying the coolness of the shade, the sharp smell of pine trees, and the sight of Pip chasing birds.

She was on the narrow path that led around the hills and into Haven. Earlier, Aunt Ellie had noticed that they were running out of • dog food. "I'll go," Molly had said immediately. "I need the walk."

Below the tallest tree in the woods, she looked at her watch. It was nearly 4:30. "I hope the pet store is open," she thought. "After all it is Memorial Day."

"If it's shut, I'll go to Marty's," Molly thought. "I can get some cans • of meat in there, at least." Marty's was the local drugstore •, and it never closed.

Pip was now at her side and a few moments later, they both stepped out of the woods and onto Haven's Main Street.

"Don't worry," she said to Pip. "We're nearly there."
She reached out to put a leash • on Pip. He, however, turned his head sharply and went running after two seagulls • on a nearby low wall. They watched him come noisily toward them. Then, stretching their long wings, they rose lazily above the wall and rooftops.
Pip and Molly watched them fly toward the woods when suddenly they changed their course and dived away, heading • instead toward the open ocean.

### Glossary

- **cans:**
- **drugstore:** store for medicine, food, etc.
- **heading:** going toward
- **leash:** piece of leather used for holding dogs
- **running out of:** (here) with almost none left
- **seagulls:** sea birds

## The Albatross

Puzzled •, Molly looked to see why. Out of the sun, a dark shape came. She narrowed her eyes. It was a falcon, perhaps the same one from the beach. Flying fast and low, it passed overhead. It then landed on the top of a warehouse beside a ship that was in the dock •.

Pip barked.

"Let's get you some food," she said. A few moments later, they arrived outside the pet store. Molly tied Pip to the railing •, and went inside.

In a building across the road from the pet store, Sergeant • Bergson moved back from the curtains and turned to Lieutenant Mundy.

"Sir, you need to take a look at this."

"What is it?" Lieutenant Mundy asked, coming to the window. He took the binoculars, and for a moment, he stopped breathing.

"What should we do, sir?"

"Get SWAT • here! Now!" roared • Dan Mundy.

## Police

**Who are the police watching with the binoculars?**
**What is SWAT?**
**What do they do?**
**Use the Internet to find out.**

---

- **dock:** water beside a pier where ships stay
- **puzzled:** not able to understand
- **railing:** fence or barrier
- **roared:** shouted very loudly
- **sergeant:** rank in police or army
- **SWAT:** Special Weapons and Tactics team

## 8 "Murder wasn't part of the deal"

Inside the store, the usual smell of straw • and small animals greeted Molly, but there was no one behind the counter •. She took two cans of dog food from the shelf. "Should I just leave the money next to the cash register •?" she wondered. Then she heard voices. They were coming from the back of the store. With the cans still in her hand, she stepped behind the counter. A door to another room was open slightly.

"Everything's fine," said a man's voice from behind the door. "We had a little problem, but everything's fine."

"A problem?" asked the other person. Molly recognized the voice: it was Mr. Hopper's, the pet store owner.

"We had to bring him back to the ship. We'll dump • his body again once we get into deeper water…"

"I don't like it. I just don't like it. Murder wasn't part of the deal…" replied Mr. Hopper.

"Shut up! You don't need to like it. I'll worry about Levy: you worry about paying me the $80,000."

Molly could hardly breathe. She had to get out of here. She had to tell her father. She had to explain what she had heard. She turned around.

A pair of green eyes stared straight at her.

"Little girls with big ears," said the man who stood in front of her, "might hear something they shouldn't."

For a second, Molly thought about rushing • past this man, but his heavy body filled the space between her and the front door completely. She took a step back.

---

### Glossary

- **cash register:** drawer for holding money
- **counter:** table where customers are served
- **dump:** throw away without care
- **rushing:** moving rapidly, urgently
- **straw:** like dry grass

## The Albatross

The man didn't move or say a word, but Molly was scared. It was his eyes, his green, narrow eyes. They were as hard and as dead as steel •.

Molly felt her heart begin to beat faster. Through the window, she could see Pip outside by the railing. He was standing and watching the man's every move. His teeth were bared •, and his ears were flat against his head.

"I was just buying some dog food… for my dog," said Molly, trying to keep her breathing normal, trying to sound brave. She held up the two cans.

The man said nothing, but his green eyes continued to stare. "Do something!" shouted some part of Molly's brain. She cast • her eyes around. Behind her, at the end of a short corridor, she saw there was another door. An exit? A storeroom •?

The man with the green eyes seemed to read her thoughts. Before Molly could move, his arm was up against the wall, blocking her way.

"Relax," he said, breathing into her face.

## Bad situation
**Have you ever been in a bad situation?**
🕬 **Tell a friend.**

---

- **bared:** uncovered
- **cast:** threw

- **steel:** kind of metal
- **storeroom:** place for boxes

# The Albatross

"Who's there?" called a voice. Molly turned as the half-open door swung sharply open. A heavy man in black pants and a black jacket stepped forward, followed by a pale-faced• Mr. Hopper.

"What are you doing here?" shouted the man in the black uniform. The man with green eyes smiled. "Following you," he said calmly.

"What's going on?" asked Mr. Hopper. Molly and he were now both behind the counter. "Who's he? And what's she doing here?" he asked, jerking• a thumb at Molly.

The two men ignored him. Instead, they stood eye to eye•, a few feet apart. From behind the counter, Molly had a good view of Pip. He was barking loudly, pulling at his leash and trying to get his head out of his collar.

"His name's Carlos," said the man in the black uniform, "and he was just leaving."

Carlos smiled again. "I don't think so," he said. "The captain and I have something to talk about."

"There's nothing we need to talk about," replied the captain.

"You're wrong," Carlos said calmly. "You see, I want you to explain the difference between $60,000 and $80,000."

"What's he talking about?" asked Hopper, leaning across the counter toward the two men. Outside, Molly saw that Pip was no longer struggling to get free. Instead, he was standing quietly, his tail moving from side to side happily. "That's strange," she thought.

"He's talking nonsense," said the captain.

Carlos's face changed. "I always knew you were a liar," he said.

Suddenly Carlos moved toward the captain. He had a knife in his hand. Just in time, the captain raised his arm and stopped Carlos's knife from plunging into his chest. The captain grabbed Carlos's wrist; and the two men began fighting, crashing into shelves and smashing into cages.

## Glossary

- **eye to eye:** face to face (suggesting conflict)
- **jerking:** moving in a quick, sudden movement
- **pale faced:** with a white face

Out of the corner of her eye, Molly saw a gray uniform outside the store... Then everything happened at once. Carlos pushed the knife toward the captain's neck; Hopper screamed; the door at the back of the store exploded; shouts filled the air; Hopper threw his hands up; the police threw the men to the ground; Molly jumped across the counter and into her father's arms. In an instant, it was over.

Molly was safely outside the store with a blanket around her shoulders, watching while Carlos, the captain and Hopper were handcuffed• and taken to three separate police cars.

Her father put his arms around her and gave her a huge hug.

"I'm fine, Dad, honestly, I am," she said, while at the same time trying to stop Pip from jumping up and licking her face.

But her father noticed her hand was shaking: a typical symptom• of shock. "Let someone check you, okay? Just for me. It'll take two minutes, I promise."

Molly was too tired to argue. "Okay," she said, handing Pip's leash to her father, "you win." Her father smiled. They were almost at the steps of the ambulance, when she glanced over her shoulder.

The police cars that were carrying Carlos, Hopper and the captain were moving slowly up Main Street, but the crowd wasn't watching them. Instead, everyone was looking at something else, something in the sky. She stopped and looked up, too.

The sky was full of falcons. They all seemed to be coming from one ship in the harbor and they were moving in all directions at once.

---

Glossary

- **handcuffed:** locked at the wrists in metal rings (typically used by police)
- **symptom:** sign

## 9 "He was dead!"

Molly sat on the edge of the bed in the back of the ambulance while the paramedic took her pulse •. From the open doors, she watched as more and more falcons rose into the sky.

"It's so strange," Molly said to her father. "Where do you think they are coming from?"

"I'm not sure," he replied, shielding • his eyes from the sun. "But I think it's something to do with the ship that I visited earlier: *The Albatross.*"

"Is it difficult for you to breathe?" the paramedic asked Molly. She shook her head.

Her father took out his phone and called a number. "Hi, Ellie, it's me," he said, and faintly • Molly could hear her aunt's voice in reply. Her father began explaining what had happened. Molly could imagine her aunt's face.

"No, she's fine..." her father was saying. "She's fine... she's fine." Molly smiled. Her father listened for a second. "Yes, okay," he said.

A moment later, when the call ended, he put his phone away and turned to Molly. "Your Aunt Ellie's coming," he said.

Molly nodded. The paramedic who had checked Molly spoke to her father. "She's had a nasty fright •," he said. "But her blood pressure, breathing, and pulse are all fine."

"Told you!" said Molly.

"Good," said her father. "Because when Aunt Ellie arrives here, I want you to go back home with her; I'm going to the docks."

"But Dad!" cried Molly. "That's not fair."

Her father smiled. "You've had enough excitement for one day."

---

### Glossary

- **faintly:** (here) opposite of loudly
- **fright:** shock; surprise
- **pulse:** beat of the heart
- **shielding:** protecting

# The Albatross

Standing on the docks beside *The Albatross*, megaphone in hand, Lieutenant Mundy held up his left hand. He was signaling to his men to wait. Situations like this always made him nervous. There were so many things that they didn't know. Would the third member of the crew give up easily? Did he have a gun? Were there others on the ship? There was only one way to find out. They had to go on board•.

"This is Lieutenant Mundy of Haven Harbor Police. Come out. We have the ship surrounded," he said. His voice boomed through the speaker and echoed off the ship's steel hull•. He waited. No response. He turned and waved his men forward. Immediately, six officers moved past him and began running along the narrow gangway onto the ship, guns in hand. Almost as soon as they were on it, they began shouting.

"Get out!" they yelled•. "Get on your knees. Get on your knees."

Slowly, a pair of hands, then a head came out of one of the stairwells• that led below the deck. Finally, a tall man emerged, his hands high in the air. It was Andre. His face was white, his eyes staring.

"No!" Andre was shouting. "He was dead. He was dead!"

In a second, the harbor police surrounded him. They pushed Andre to the ground and handcuffed him, but still the man continued.

"I saw him. I saw him. I saw him," he moaned•.

**Guess**
Who is Andre talking about?

---

- **moaned:** said making a low sad sound
- **on board:** onto the ship
- **yelled:** shouted
- **stairwells:** spaces where stairs are built
- **steel hull:** metal body of a ship

47

"Lieutenant Mundy!" called Sergeant Bergson. He was at the bottom of the stairwell that Andre had come up. "You need to take a look at this."

Lieutenant Mundy stepped quickly into the stairwell and went below deck. Sergeant Bergson and two more officers were standing in front of the door to the hold. Although the lights inside it were switched on, it was still almost dark. Lieutenant Mundy switched on his flashlight and stepped through the doorway.

This time, the scene was very different. This time, the boxes were no longer in neat rows •. "Looks like there's been a fight," he thought. But that wasn't the biggest difference. There, at the end of the hold, beyond the messy piles of boxes on the floor, lay a half-open door through which a bright light was shining. And now everything made sense to him. The hold was smaller than normal. He had been correct. The reason for that was simple. There was a false wall • that separated one part of the hold from the other.

He drew his gun and signaled silently for one of his men to go left and for one to go right. He, Sergeant Bergson, and the others moved slowly forward. With every step closer, the men could see how much the false wall resembled the real walls of the hold. It was made of thin wood, but painted exactly the same color as the real hold. In fact, without the door being open, no one would ever know the secret room was there.

All four of them reached the false wall and lined up with their backs against it. With his gun in his right hand, Lieutenant Mundy started a countdown with the fingers of his left hand…3 …2 …1.

---

### Glossary

- **false wall:** not real; wall that hides something behind it
- **rows:** columns; vertical lines

48

First Lieutenant Mundy followed by Sergeant Bergson and then the other two officers dashed through the door, their bodies tense, their guns ready.

There, in the small room, among empty birdcages, lay the body of an old man, his face turned away from them, his clothes damp, his gray hair sticking to his skull.

Lieutenant Mundy knelt down and reached for the man's wrist. He pressed his fingers to the main vein. The man's skin felt ice cold. Lieutenant Mundy began loosening his fingers, preparing to drop the old man's wrist. But then he felt it, the faintest of pulses.

"Get an ambulance," he shouted. "He's still alive."

### Old man
**Can you remember everything that happened to this old man? Go back to the text and check.**

### Glossary
- **damp:** a little wet
- **dashed:** rushed; moved quickly
- **faintest:** smallest; lightest
- **skull:** bone in the head

## 10 "The shoes!"

Molly came to Haven Hospital for the first time when she was nine years old. She had fallen off her bike and landed badly. A cut • had appeared on her chin and bled onto her new T-shirt. When she arrived home, her mother had wrapped • her in a yellow towel from the bathroom. Then, calmly, she had driven Molly to Haven Hospital. She could still remember her mother's warm hand around her; the yellow towel turning red; the hospital doors opening and the smell greeting her for the first time.

The next time she went to the hospital, the same smell greeted her. This time, her mother was having treatment • for her cancer •. Molly had tried to hold her breath • for as long as she could. It was a silly game. A month later, when her mother died, Molly had held her breath for two minutes.

Today, she was in the hospital once again, surrounded by the same familiar, sharp smell that she hated. She was in an elevator climbing to the sixth floor •. A nurse who was carrying charts • was standing in front of her, his face to the doors. Beside her, her father stood in his gray uniform, gun by his side. This time she and her father were on police business. This time, Molly wasn't holding her breath.

## Smell

**Can you think of a place that has a particular smell?**

▷◁ **Tell a friend.**

---

- **breath:** air we take in
- **cancer:** disease
- **charts:** information sheets
- **cut:** injury that causes bleeding
- **floor:** level in a building
- **treatment:** medical care
- **wrapped:** covered in

The elevator's doors opened and a tall woman, with long dark hair, stepped forward and introduced herself. "My name's Dr. Afreen. I believe you're here to see Mr. Andreas," she said and gave Molly a smile.

"That's right," replied Molly's father. They began walking along the corridor.

"Has he said anything since he came in?"

"He's been unconscious• the whole time," replied Dr. Afreen.

Molly's father nodded. "That's okay. We know a little about him from one of the others on the ship. Seems Mr. Andreas was the engineer on board. He discovered his crew mates were trying to smuggle rare birds and threatened to call the police."

The doctor shook her head. "So they decided to kill him?"

"Yeah," replied Molly's father. "They threw him overboard, but he turned up• on the beach. That's when my daughter, Molly, saw him..."

"How terrible for you," the doctor said, her sparkling hazel• eyes falling on Molly.

"They brought him back to the ship and put him in the hold. They were waiting until they were in deep water to throw him in the ocean again..." continued Molly's father.

"Awful," said the doctor quietly.

"I just need Molly to formally identify him. Make sure that he was the man she saw on the beach. Is that okay?'

"Sure," said Dr. Afreen and she opened the door and led them into the room.

"It's him," said Molly quietly when she saw the old man in the bed.

---

Glossary

- **hazel:** greenish brown
- **turned up:** appeared
- **unconscious:** asleep

"Are you absolutely sure it's the old man you saw on the beach?" her father asked.

Molly nodded.

"Okay," said Molly's father, putting an arm around her. "I think we are done here •. Thank you for your time."

"You're welcome," said Dr. Afreen, shutting the door and stepping out into the corridor once again with Molly and her father.

"I'll come back when Mr. Andreas has regained consciousness •," said Molly's father, but just as Dr. Afreen was about to answer, an announcement sounded: "Dr. Afreen, please report to Room 67. Dr. Afreen to Room 67, please."

She shrugged her shoulders. "Sorry, I've gotta • go," she said and she began hurrying down the corridor. "Nice meeting you," she said.

Molly and her father watched her go. "She's nice," said Molly. "Don't you think?"

Her father smiled, but said nothing. They began walking toward the elevators again. Molly noticed that the hospital smell seemed even stronger in the corridors than in the patients' rooms. Just then, her father's cell phone rang.

"Hello?" said her father. There was a pause while he listened to the voice on the other end. "You gotta be kidding me •!" he said suddenly, almost shouting. "Never mind how it happened, we'll sort that out later. Right now, we have to concentrate on finding him…"

What was he talking about? What was happening?

"… and I want road blocks on Highway 12 and I want CCTV footage • of the area…" continued her father.

Molly noticed a man coming along the corridor toward them. He was carrying a bouquet of flowers so large that it covered most of his face. She didn't pay much attention to him, but she did happen to glance • at his feet. What she saw puzzled her.

---

### Glossary

- **are done here:** are finished
- **CCTV footage:** security camera film
- **consciousness:** awareness
- **glance:** look quickly
- **gotta:** got to; must
- **kidding me:** having a joke; not serious

# The Albatross

Her father's phone call ended and they continued walking to the elevator.

"Unbelievable," her father said angrily.

"What's up?" asked Molly as the elevator arrived.

Her father let out an angry sigh•. "It's Carlos. He was let out of the police station," he said, watching the elevator doors open.

"Carlos…? But how?" asked Molly. They stepped into the elevator.

"A clerical error•. He was misidentified• and released by mistake…" replied her father, pressing the button for the floor that was marked 'G'. "He was in jail," he continued, "and he just walked out…" The elevator doors began to close. Between the closing doors, the view of the corridor became thinner and thinner and thinner…

Suddenly, straight as a sword, Molly thrust• her arm between the closing doors. For a second, Molly's arm was crushed• painfully and she cried out. Then the doors reversed their direction and once again, the corridor was fully visible.

"The shoes!" Molly said, rubbing her arm and stepping out of the elevator. "The man, that passed us in the corridor holding the big bouquet of flowers – he didn't have any laces• in his shoes…"
Her father looked at her as though she were talking nonsense. "Like in jail," she said, "Like in jail!"

- **clerical error:** mistake in documents
- **crushed:** squeezed together
- **laces:** long, thin pieces of fabric for tightening shoes
- **misidentified:** incorrectly recognized
- **sigh:** long, deep breath
- **thrust:** pushed hard

55

## 11 "If I am cursed, then he is lucky"

"If I were you, I wouldn't do that," said Lieutenant Mundy.

Two blazing green eyes turned and stared at the gun that was now pointing straight at them.

"Drop it," Lieutenant Mundy said in a low voice. "Now!"

Slowly, Carlos brought the pillow• away from the old man's face. When the pillow was past the edge of the bed, he released it. It fell from his hands and landed with a soft thud• beside the bouquet of flowers that already lay on the ground.

"Step away from him, nice and slow."

Carlos, eyes still fixed on the gun, moved a few feet away from the bed in which Levy lay. As he did so, he cast a glance at the window on the wall of the other side of the bed.

Lieutenant Mundy smiled. "I won't stop you…" he said, "although I should remind you that we are six floors up. "Now get on your knees and put your hands on your head. Now!"

Carlos's body became as tense as a spring. But Lieutenant Mundy could read his thoughts. This man with green wolf-like eyes was calculating his chances of attacking him and getting the gun.

"If you're a gambling• man," said Lieutenant Mundy calmly, "then go ahead and try…"

Reluctantly•, Carlos dropped to one knee, and then two. He raised his hands and placed them on top of his head.

"Cross your legs behind you," ordered Lieutenant Mundy. "Do it!"

With his gun pointed steadily• at Carlos, Lieutenant Mundy reached for the handcuffs that he always carried in his belt.

---

### Glossary

- **gambling:** taking a chance
- **pillow:** soft object; we rest our heads on it
- **reluctantly:** not really wanting to
- **steadily:** without moving
- **thud:** dull, heavy noise

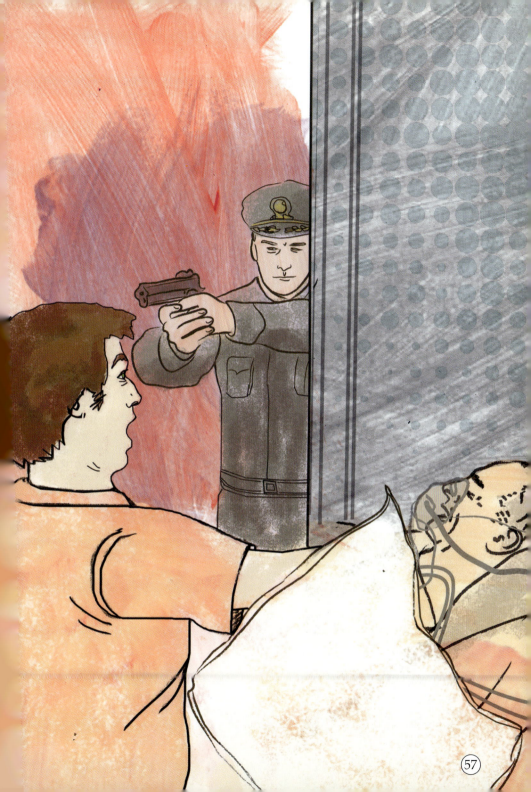

As he did so, three hospital security officers burst• through the door behind him. Within moments, Carlos was securely handcuffed, and lying flat on the ground. The three security officers were standing over him waiting for the reinforcements• that Lieutenant Mundy had called for. While Lieutenant Mundy was reading Carlos his rights•, Dr. Afreen came running into the room, followed by Molly. She ran to her father and hugged him tightly.

"Is he okay? Did he hurt him?" asked Dr. Afreen, checking the machines around her patient and feeling for his pulse.

But before anyone could answer her, Carlos began laughing. He was laughing so hard that he could hardly breathe. "Hurt him? Ha! Ha! Ha! Twice," he coughed•, "I have tried to kill him twice… Ha! Ha! Ha!" He was laughing so hard he curled into a ball. "If I am cursed•, then he is lucky! Ha! Ha! Ha!"

"Let's hope he finds jail just as funny," Lieutenant Mundy said.

## Lucky

**Do you believe that some people are lucky?**

**Discuss in small groups.**

### Glossary

- **burst:** rushed in
- **coughed:** moved air out of his lungs sharply
- **cursed:** always having bad luck
- **reinforcements:** extra police officers
- **rights:** legal privileges

## 12 "My wife's name was Karis"

 A week after Carlos had tried to kill Levy for the second time, Levy Andreas woke up. Dr. Afreen immediately called Haven police department. As soon as he heard that the old man was well enough to be interviewed •, Molly's father called his daughter and together they went back to the hospital.

"I'd like to ask him a few questions. Is that okay?" said Molly's father. They were on the sixth floor again and Dr. Afreen had met them outside Levy's room as soon as they had arrived.

"Sure," said Dr. Afreen. "He's just finished eating, so let's go in."

Inside, the old man was lying in bed. He turned his head toward them as they came in.

"Mr. Andreas, this is Lieutenant Mundy of Haven Harbor Police and this is his daughter, Molly," said Dr. Afreen. "They'd like to speak to you for a little while. Is that alright?"

The old man's eyes looked empty for a moment. Though his gray hair was neatly brushed, he looked very tired. His face was thin and his lips were dry. Finally, he nodded his head. "Yes, yes. That's fine," he said, his voice not more than a whisper.

"Hello, Mr. Andreas," said Molly's father. "How are you?"

The old man smiled. "I'm still here," he said quietly.

Molly's father smiled, too. "Sir, what's the last thing you remember about *The Albatross*?"

"*The Albatross*?" said the old man. He swallowed. Molly stepped forward and began pouring some water from the jug • at the side of his bed into a glass.

---

- **be interviewed:** when you ask someone questions

- **jug:**

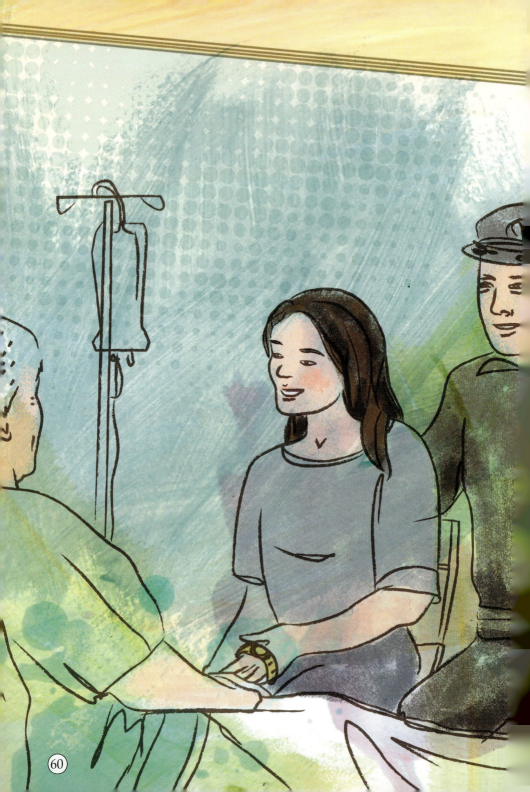

# The Albatross

"Do you remember *The Albatross*?" asked her father.

The old man shook his head very slightly. Molly gave him the glass, he drank and thanked Molly with a nod.

"I don't remember," said the old man. "I don't remember anything."

"Do you remember Carlos? The captain? Andre?" asked her father. The old man shook his head.

"Don't worry, Mr. Andreas," said the doctor, replacing• her chart. "Sometimes it can take a little while for your memory to return fully•."

Molly was looking at her father. He understood her unspoken question and he nodded.

Molly took the watch out of her pocket. Its hands were still stuck at 1:38. She handed it to the old man, who took it hesitantly.

"To my darling Leveros 'Levy' Andreas," he said, reading the inscription and translating it into English. "All my love, K."

From outside, the sound of an approaching• ambulance filled the air. It grew closer and closer to the hospital until the siren stopped suddenly, doors slammed and urgent voices called out.

Something else was happening. Molly could see that the old man's lip had begun to tremble•. Slowly, his face was changing, becoming less confused, less uncertain.

When he finally spoke, tears clouded• his eyes.

"Karis," he said. "My wife's name was Karis."

## Glossary

- **approaching:** coming closer
- **clouded:** (here) filled
- **fully:** completely
- **replacing:** (here) putting back in its place
- **tremble:** shake (because very emotional)

# 13 "Eventually, we feel grateful"

They were sitting in Levy's hospital room. Molly was on the chair and Levy on the bed with his legs swinging below him. They were waiting for one of the assistants to bring a wheelchair • to take Levy to the hospital's front door. Finally, after nearly a month of treatment, today was Levy's last day in the hospital. He was happier than Molly had ever seen him. "I'm fine. I can walk to the door," Levy had objected, but the head nurse wasn't listening. "Rules are rules," she said.

From outside the window, a beam of sunlight fell into the room and lay across Levy's shoulders and chest. He was dressed in a new, dark blue shirt and a pair of jeans.

"Crazy," said Levy, smiling. "I'm fit • now. I don't need a wheelchair!" he said again.

Molly nodded. She had to admit the rule about wheelchairs did seem strange. Was this really the same man that she had seen on the beach just a few weeks ago? "No running when we get outside, okay?" said Molly.

Levy laughed. "Yes, miss," he replied, his brown eyes twinkling • .

They sat in silence for a few moments, each thinking their own thoughts. Molly knew she was going to miss him. She had visited Levy on all the twenty-six days he had been in the hospital, except one. When the soccer team bus broke down two weeks ago on the journey back from a match in upstate • New York, she had called him instead.

"Do you still miss her?" Levy asked suddenly.

They had talked about lots of things: Levy's home town of Nikiti and its view of the Aegean Sea; Levy's house; Molly's father; her soccer team; her coach's tactics • ; and her friends. But it was Molly's mother and Levy's wife that they had discussed the least. Molly didn't need to ask who 'her' was. She nodded.

## Glossary

- **fit:** healthy
- **tactics:** carefully planned actions
- **twinkling:** shining
- **upstate:** northern part (of state)
- **wheelchair:** chair with wheels

# The Albatross

"How old were you?" he asked.

"Almost fourteen," Molly replied. "She died two days before my birthday."

"It's not easy: grief •, I mean. At first, it is impossible. You understand?"

Molly nodded again.

"But slowly, the good things, the things that you loved about that person fill the emptiness. Eventually, we feel…" he stopped, trying to search for the best word.

"Grateful?" Molly offered.

"Yes. Grateful. That's exactly right, Molly. We feel it because we have known that person. You see, everything ends, Molly, but the trick is to appreciate the things we have when we have them."

"Did you always feel like that?" Molly asked. "I mean, grateful for Karis?"

Levy laughed. "It took me a long time to understand, too long. Some people understand it immediately. With others, it takes longer…"

Molly thought about her father. She wondered if he would ever feel the same as Levy did…as she did.

## Grief

**Has someone important in your life died?
How did you feel?**

📢 **Tell a friend.**

---

• **grief:** sadness (because of a death)

"But listen," said Levy, his face breaking into a smile again, "let's not be sad. We are here, we are healthy, and we have friends and family."

"Hello, you two!" said Dr. Afreen, coming into the room.

Levy turned around. "Doctor! Welcome. Molly and I were just chatting."

Dr. Afreen smiled. "Some things never change," she said and gave Molly a wink•. "You are going to wear your lungs out•, Mr. Andreas."

Levy laughed. "Don't worry, Doctor, they are still strong."

Dr. Afreen smiled and signed the chart that lay hanging at the bottom of the bed. "So, back to Greece?" she asked, pushing a strand• of her long, dark hair from her face.

"Yes, back home," replied Levy. "I have a brother in Nikiti, nieces and nephews, and a house that I want to buy. My brother and I have a little boat. We'll fish, we'll sell our catch•… You must come, Doctor, you and Molly."

Before Dr. Afreen could answer, the assistant came into the room, pushing a wheelchair.

"Ah," said Dr. Afreen, "your transport has arrived." Levy shook his head and sat down in it. Dr. Afreen shook Levy's hand. "It's been a pleasure knowing you, Mr. Andreas. I wish you all the best•. Perhaps I'll make it to• Nikiti one of these days, who knows?"

## Glossary

- **all the best:** best wishes
- **catch:** all the fish in a net
- **make it to:** travel to; visit
- **strand:** single hair
- **wear your lungs out:** feel tired (because of talking so much)
- **wink:** when you quickly close one eye to show you are joking

## 14 "It's been a long time"

"So, what did you think of the show?" asked Molly's father.

They were standing in Times Square in New York City, next to a hotdog stand •. Molly nodded and chewed for a second, her mouth full of hotdog, pickles, and mustard. She swallowed.

"It was awesome •," she said. "Thanks, Dad. It was the best birthday present ever."

They had just been to see a show on Broadway. It was a surprise birthday treat • for Molly. Her father had given her the tickets that morning. What a way to celebrate her seventeenth birthday!

# The Albatross

They walked up Broadway and toward Columbus Circle. They both noticed a Greek flag hanging up outside a restaurant. Molly stared as they went past. Her father looked, too. They said nothing, but each one remembered that day a year ago.

"You look tired," said her father eventually. "You want to take a cab • ?"

Molly nodded. They stopped and faced the oncoming • traffic.

"How's Levy?" asked her father, raising his arm and watching three yellow cabs rush past. Levy had returned to the United States to be a witness • in the trial • of the captain and the crew of The Albatross. After the sentences were passed • and the crew was put in prison, he had come to Haven and spent a few days there with them. Molly and he had continued to keep in contact with emails and cards.

"He's good," replied Molly. "He and his brother have just bought a larger boat. They called it…"

"Molly?" asked her father, eyes on the traffic.

Molly smiled. "Karis," she said.

Just then, a yellow cab turned sharply and pulled up beside them.

"Riverside Drive, West 91st • ," said her father through the open window. The cab driver nodded. Molly and her father climbed in and the cab pulled quickly into the traffic again. They were on their way to Molly's grandparents' apartment. For the first time since her mother had died, three years ago now, she and her father were going to stay with them.

Molly looked at her father's face. She decided that he looked tired; perhaps even a little tense. She knew it was painful for her father going back to the grandparent's apartment, remembering her mother. But it was good to remember her and she never forgot Levy's advice: be grateful.

## Glossary

- **awesome:** amazing; fantastic
- **cab:** taxi
- **oncoming:** approaching; coming toward them
- **sentences were passed:** punishments were given
- **stand:** (here) small vehicle from which food is sold
- **treat:** surprise; special present
- **trial:** court case; legal action
- **West 91st.** West ninety first (name of street)
- **witness:** person who tells the court about a crime

Molly took her father's hand and squeezed it. Her father turned to her smiling. "What was that for?" he asked.

"Thanks," Molly simply said. "Thanks for everything, Dad."

The cab stopped and her father paid. "Have a good evening, guys," said the taxi driver, smiling.

Outside, arm-in-arm, Molly and her father paused in front of the tall apartment block.

"It's been a long time..." said her father, looking up. Molly looked up, too.

On and on, shining out like stars, the lights from a thousand different rooms rose in front of them.

Her father took a deep breath. Molly smiled at him; and together, they stepped forward.

# BEFORE READING
## Personal Response

**1  Read and answer the following questions on your own or with a partner.**

**a)** Did you enjoy the story? Which chapter did you enjoy the most?

**b)** Which character was the most important in the story?

**c)** Do you know someone who is as old as Levy?
Describe him/her.

**d)** Part of the story takes part on a big ship.
Have you ever traveled on one?
If you have, tell your classmates about it.
Where did you go?
Did you feel seasick?
Was it a long trip?
Would you go again?

**e)** Discuss the role and importance of the different pets in the story:
Herman and Pip.

**f)** Do you think people should be allowed to have rare animals
as pets?

**g)** In your opinion, who deserves the longest prison sentence?
(Choose between Carlos, Hopper, Andre or the captain.)

# AFTER READING

## Comprehension

**1 Check (✔) true (T) or false (F).**

|  | | T | F |
|---|---|---|---|
| **a)** | Levy was a cook on a ship called *The Albatross*. | ☐ | ☐ |
| **b)** | After Levy finished the voyage, he planned to retire and live in the United States. | ☐ | ☐ |
| **c)** | One night, Levy found rare birds called falcons in the ship's hold. | ☐ | ☐ |
| **d)** | Levy didn't know that the captain planned to sell the falcons to a man called Hopper. | ☐ | ☐ |
| **e)** | Levy fell into the ocean by accident. | ☐ | ☐ |
| **f)** | Molly Mundy's dog found Levy lying on the beach. | ☐ | ☐ |
| **g)** | Molly Mundy's father found a gold watch with an inscription on it. | ☐ | ☐ |
| **h)** | Andre collected Levy's body from the beach and brought it to the ship again. | ☐ | ☐ |
| **i)** | Molly Mundy's father inspected *The Albatross* when it arrived in Haven. | ☐ | ☐ |
| **j)** | The falcons escaped from *The Albatross* because Andre released them. | ☐ | ☐ |

**2 Correct the false sentences in Exercise 1.**

**3 Did these events happen on the ship (S) or on land (L)? Check (✔).**

|  | | S | L |
|---|---|---|---|
| **a)** | Lieutenant Mundy questioned the captain. | ☐ | ☐ |
| **b)** | The captain was arrested and handcuffed. | ☐ | ☐ |
| **c)** | Molly stopped the elevator. | ☐ | ☐ |
| **d)** | Lieutenant Mundy pointed a gun at Carlos for the second time. | ☐ | ☐ |
| **e)** | Andre was handcuffed by the police. | ☐ | ☐ |

**4 Why did these characters do these things? Match the question with the correct answer.**

a) At the start of the story, how did Levy know that Andre was in the hold?

b) Why did Levy go to see the captain?

c) Why did Levy not sink to the bottom of the ocean

d) Why did Carlos dislike the captain?

e) Why did Pip suddenly look happy when he was outside the pet store and Molly was inside?

f) Why did Levy release all of the falcons?

g) Why did Carlos have a pillow in his hands when he was in Levy's hospital room?

h) Why did Carlos call Levy "lucky?"

1 ☐ He wanted to attract the police's attention to the ship.

2 ☐ He was tied with ropes and they weren't heavy enough.

3 ☐ He had survived many attempts to kill him.

4 ☐ He wanted him to call the police.

5 ☐ He wanted to use it to kill Levy.

6 ☐ He didn't trust him with the money.

7 ☐ He found an apple core belonging to him.

8 ☐ He saw Molly's father.

**5 Can you remember these details from the story? Circle the correct answer.**

a) Levy had spent nearly **(50 / 55 / 60)** years at sea.

b) Levy's gold watch was a present from his wife on his **(40th / 50th / 60th)** birthday.

c) The ship's cat was called **(Harold / Herman / Henry)**.

d) There were nearly **(30 / 40 / 50)** cages in the hold.

e) When Molly woke up on Memorial Day Monday, the time was exactly **(6 / 7 / 8)** A.M.

f) When Molly found the gold watch, the time on it was **(1:32 / 1:35 / 1:38)**.

71

# AFTER READING
## Characters

**1** **Match the brief descriptions below with the correct character. Write 'M' for Molly, 'L' for Levy, 'H' for Hopper.**

a) ☐ likes soccer.

b) ☐ has a dog named Pip.

c) ☐ is a store owner.

d) ☐ will soon retire.

e) ☐ is a criminal.

f) ☐ wants to buy a small boat.

g) ☐ was married to Karis.

h) ☐ is arrested.

i) ☐ is sixteen at the beginning of the story.

**2** **Who said it? Write Andre, Carlos, Molly, Hopper, or Dan Mundy.**

> I don't like it.
> I just don't like it. Murder wasn't part of the deal.

a) .....................................

> I was just buying some dog food... for my dog.

b) .....................................

> I always knew you were a liar.

c) .....................................

> He was dead! He was dead!

d) .....................................

> I want road blocks on Highway 12 and CCTV footage of the area.

e) .....................................

> If I am cursed, then he is lucky.

f) .....................................

72

**3 Complete the table with the correct names and adjectives.**

> **characters:** the captain  Carlos  Molly  Levy  Andre
> **adjectives:** unintelligent  greedy  resourceful  violent  strong

| Character | Adjective | Reason |
|---|---|---|
| Molly's father | is smart | because he suspected the captain immediately. |
| a) ........................... | is ........................... | because he fought with the captain and tried to kill Levy several times. |
| b) ........................... | is ........................... | because he tried to cheat Carlos and Andre. |
| c) ........................... | is ........................... | because he survived. |
| d) ........................... | is ........................... | because he made several stupid mistakes. |
| e) ........................... | is ........................... | because she used the internet to find out more about the watch. |

**4 Work with a partner and discuss the following.**

**a)** Do you think Levy is a sociable person or not?

**b)** Do you think Molly is a brave person or not?

73

# AFTER READING

## Plot and Theme

**1 Put these sentences about the story in the correct order.**

| 1 | 2 | 3 | 4 | 5 | 6 | 7 | 8 |
|---|---|---|---|---|---|---|---|
|   |   |   |   |   |   |   |   |

a) Carlos held the bouquet of flowers tightly in his hand, trying to cover his face.

b) Levy pulled the sheet away. He couldn't believe his eyes: a falcon!

c) 'You aren't going to like this,' thought Andre and handed the binoculars to Carlos.

d) 'That's strange,' thought Molly, watching the falcon as it flew over the beach.

e) Slowly, with a pillow in his hand, Carlos moved toward the old man in the bed.

f) With a mouth full of hotdog, pickles, and mustard, Molly smiled at her father.

g) When the assistant brought the wheelchair, Levy didn't argue. He just sat down.

h) Molly jumped across the pet store's counter and into her father's arms.

**2 These three things are in the story. Say why they are important.**

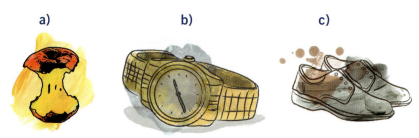

a)   b)   c)

**3 Why did it happen? Think about these events from the story and explain them to your partner. You may have to use your own ideas.**

a) Levy wanted the captain to call the police when he discovered the falcons.

b) When Levy left the captain's cabin with the falcon, the captain called someone.

c) Molly was unhappy when she woke up early on Monday morning.

d) When Molly saw the falcon flying toward Haven, she was puzzled.

e) Carlos and Andre probably threw Levy into the ocean at 1:38 A.M.

f) At first, Molly didn't see Levy lying on the beach.

g) Although Carlos told Andre to put chains around Levy's body, he didn't do it.

h) When Molly, her father, and the police and medical services arrived on the beach, there was no dead body.

**4 Complete these sentences with your own ideas and then discuss them with a partner.**

a) Molly couldn't understand the inscription on the gold watch that she found because .................................................................................

b) At first, Molly's father thought that Molly made up a story about a body on the beach, but he changed his mind after he spoke to the captain because .................................................................................

c) Carlos told Andre to bring Levy back to the ship when they saw his body on the beach because .................................................................................

d) When Levy saw the gold watch in the hospital, he was upset but it actually helped him because .................................................................................

**5 Think about the following questions and discuss them with your class.**

a) Who did Molly visit in the hospital when she was younger?

b) Why did Levy call his boat *Karis*?

c) Why did Levy and Molly talk about grief?

75

# AFTER READING

## Language

1 **Complete the questions with the passive form of the verbs then answer the questions.**

   a) Who / Levy's watch / find by ?
   ..................................................................................................
   ..................................................................................................

   b) When / the falcons / discover ?
   ..................................................................................................
   ..................................................................................................

   c) Why / the falcons / smuggle ?
   ..................................................................................................
   ..................................................................................................

   d) How many / times / Levy / nearly kill by Carlos ?
   ..................................................................................................
   ..................................................................................................

   e) What / Carlos's face / in hospital corridor / cover by ?
   ..................................................................................................
   ..................................................................................................

2 **Read the sentences and report what the characters said.**

What was the new engineer's name?

Leveros Andreas, but we called him Levy.

Has he said anything since he came in?

He's been unconscious the whole time.

**3** **Match the expressions from the story with their meanings.**

a) It was awesome.                1 ☐ I can't believe what you are saying.
b) You gotta be kidding me!       2 ☐ What's happening?
c) I think we're done here.       3 ☐ It was amazing.
d) What's up?                     4 ☐ I haven't been a good parent.
e) I haven't been there for you.  5 ☐ We have finished.

**4** **Put the words in italics in order to complete the sentences.**

a) If the police find the falcons, *mean / it / will / us / for / trouble / all / of*

.................................................................................................................. .

b) If the police find Levy's body, *the / spend / in / 20 / will / next / years / prison / we*

.................................................................................................................. .

c) If the pet store is closed, *will / I / to / Marty's / go*

.................................................................................................................. .

d) If I am cursed, *he / lucky / then / is*

.................................................................................................................. .

e) If I were you, *would / and / I / pillow / drop / that / away / move / it / from*

.................................................................................................................. .

**5 Complete the sentences using the correct verb form.**

a) The captain probably called Carlos and ........... (tell) him about Levy's discovery.
b) Carlos and Andre ........... (fight) with Levy. Then Andre carried his body to the deck and ........... (throw) him overboard.
c) At exactly seven o'clock in the morning, Molly ........... (wake) up, ........... (get) out of bed, and rubbed her eyes. She ........... (feel) terrible.
d) Molly ........... (be) on the beach when she looked up and ........... (see) a falcon.
e) Molly ........... (begin) walking toward Pip, who ........... (bark) loudly.
f) When Molly reached the tree trunk, she ........... (find) the body that ........... (lie) behind it.

77

# AFTER READING

## Exit Test

**P** 1 **Read and choose the correct answers.**

**a)** Levy finds the falcons
  **1** ☐ by chance.
  **2** ☐ because he was searching for them.
  **3** ☐ in the captain's cabin.
  **4** ☐ deliberately.

**b)** Andre and Carlos throw Levy overboard because Levy
  **1** ☐ lost one of their falcons.
  **2** ☐ discovered their secret.
  **3** ☐ argued with the captain.
  **4** ☐ slipped and fell.

**c)** When Molly returns to the beach with her father, he
  **1** ☐ sees a falcon.
  **2** ☐ doesn't want to speak to Molly.
  **3** ☐ thinks Molly didn't really see a body.
  **4** ☐ is angry with Molly.

**d)** Dan Mundy realizes Molly was telling the truth when
  **1** ☐ he learns that the ship is carrying TVs.
  **2** ☐ the captain tells him about Levy's accident.
  **3** ☐ the captain becomes nervous.
  **4** ☐ he speaks to Dr. Afreen.

**e)** Carlos follows the captain to Hopper's store because
  **1** ☐ he wants his share of the $60,000 immediately.
  **2** ☐ he wants to see what Hooper looks like.
  **3** ☐ he doesn't trust the captain.
  **4** ☐ he wants to buy dog food.

**2** **Listen to a news report about** *The Albatross* **and complete the form below.**

| | |
|---|---|
| Name of ship | The Albatross |
| Type of ship | a) .......................................... |
| People originally on the ship | b) .......................................... |
| | c) .......................................... |
| | d) .......................................... |
| | e) .......................................... |
| Time of arrival | f) .......................................... |
| Place of arrival | Haven |
| Registered cargo type | g) .......................................... TVs |
| Other cargo found on ship | h) .......................................... |

**3 Can you remember the words from the story to label the picture?**

# AFTER READING
## Project

### Endangered birds

1 The Saker falcon is an example of an endangered bird. Use the words to complete the text below.

beautiful  birds  illegally  lives  number  nests

The Saker falcon usually ................. on open, grassy areas. It eats rats, mice, and other ................. such as pigeon. It often lives in old ................. that were made by other birds. It lays between 3 - 6 eggs. The ................. of Saker falcons is falling because it is losing its habitat and because more people are catching and selling it ................. . There are probably less than 8,000 of these ................. birds still in the wild.

 2 Use the Internet to find similar information about two other endangered birds. Find out which charities protect birds. Show your project to the class.

### Birds as symbols

 1 Which countries have these birds as their national symbol? Do some research and find out.
- peacock
- kiwi
- golden eagle
- gallic rooster
- emu
- Saker falcon

2 If you could choose a bird to be the symbol of your classroom or your school, what would you choose? Make some suggestions and take a vote.